JUNKO TABEI

MASTERS THE MOUNTAINS

REBEL GiRLS

Our books are available at special quantity discounts for bulk purchase for sale promotions, premiums, fundraising, and educational needs. For details, write to sales@rebelgirls.co

Editorial Director: Elena Favilli
Art Director: Giulia Flamini
Text: Nancy Ohlin
Cover and Illustrations: Montse Galbany
Cover Lettering: Cesar Yannarella
Graphic design: Annalisa Ventura
Printed in Italy by Graphicom

This is a work of historical fiction. We have tried to be as accurate as possible, but names, characters, businesses, places, events, locales, and incidents may have been changed to suit the needs of the story.

www.rebelgirls.co

First Edition
ISBN 978-1-7333292-0-0

MORE BOOKS
FROM REBEL GIRLS . . .

Good Night Stories for Rebel Girls

•

Good Night Stories for Rebel Girls 2

•

I Am a Rebel Girl:
A Journal to Start Revolutions

•

Ada Lovelace Cracks the Code

•

Madam C. J. Walker Builds a Business

•

Dr. Wangari Maathai Plants a Forest

To the Rebel Girls of the world...

**No mountain is too high
if you put one foot in front
of the other.**

Junko Tabei

September 22, 1939-October 20, 2016

Japan

CHAPTER ONE

"Who wants to go on a field trip to the mountains?" Mr. Watanabe asked his fourth-grade class.

Junko's hand shot up in the air. She wasn't sure why, since going to the mountains probably meant lots of hiking and climbing, and she was bad at sports. *Really* bad. PE was her least favorite subject at school. She couldn't do the gymnastics other kids could do, and she much preferred reading to running.

This is not a good idea, she thought. She lowered her hand and pretended to sweep her bangs out of her eyes. But she really did want to try. It sounded like fun. She raised her hand again and made herself keep it there. Her heart thumped wildly in her chest.

The teacher nodded and smiled at her. "Ms. Ishibashi. Excellent. Anyone else?"

Other students raised their hands, too. Two boys sitting in front of Junko smirked and whispered to each other. She could guess what

they were saying: *There's no way Junko can climb a mountain. She's tiny and weak. Plus, she's a girl.*

"Gentlemen, do you have something you'd like to share with the class?" Mr. Watanabe asked.

"No, sir!" The two boys sat up straight in their seats.

"That's good to hear! And since it seems like enough of you are interested in doing some

mountaineering, I'll contact your parents and organize the details for our trip this summer."

Junko squirmed. *Mountaineering.* The word made it sound so serious. She was nervous but also excited.

After school, she walked home with her friend Hideo. They followed a path along the river, like they always did. Colorful petals from flowering fruit trees rained down around them from above.

"Just ignore those guys," Hideo said. He must have noticed the whispering in class.

"I'll try," Junko said, still a little nervous about the trip. "Have you ever done any mountaineering?"

"Yeah, on Castle Mountain," Hideo joked. Junko laughed with her friend. Castle Mountain wasn't really a mountain. It was more like a hill, and it was in the middle of their town, Miharu, in north-central Japan. From the top, you could see the whole town—farms, temples, houses, shops, and even their elementary school.

Junko had hiked up Castle Mountain a bunch of times with Hideo and her other friends. She liked seeing the world from up high.

But Castle Mountain wasn't *that* high. It was small, just like Junko herself. The mountain Mr. Watanabe wanted to take them to would surely be much bigger. From the top, you could probably see all of Japan.

~

That night at dinner, Junko told her family about the field trip.

"Are you sure you want to go, Jun-chan?" her mother, Kiyo, asked. She ladled steaming white rice into a blue earthenware bowl, added a pickled plum, and passed the bowl to Junko. "It doesn't seem like your sort of thing."

"Well, *I* think it sounds like quite the adventure," her father, Morinobu, said as he lifted a piece of grilled mackerel with his chopsticks. Behind his glasses, his brown eyes were cheerful.

Around the crowded table, everyone began talking at once: Junko's brothers and sisters, the two housekeepers who lived with them, and some of her father's employees from his printing company, who also lived with them.

"Will it be Mount Fuji? Or Mount Kita? Or some other mountain?"

"My friend climbed Mount Fuji once."

"What if you run into a bear?"

"What if you run into lots of bears?"

"What if everyone reaches the top except for you?"

"Yeah, didn't you flunk gym class?"

"Isn't mountain climbing a man's sport?"

Junko lowered her head and concentrated on her rice as the conversation swirled around her. She was the second youngest of seven children, and she often got lost in her thoughts. The pickled plum was extra-salty and sour, the way she liked it, but she barely noticed. She was too busy answering questions in her head.

Why shouldn't *girls climb mountains? This is 1949, not medieval times,* she thought. *And so what if I'm not a super-duper-mega-athlete? I can still put one foot in front of the other. If I have to take tons of breaks, or if I'm the last one to reach the top, that's fine. At least I'll have tried my best.*

Junko trusted Mr. Watanabe, who was her favorite teacher. Actually, he was pretty much *everyone's* favorite teacher. He was different from the other instructors at their school, and it wasn't just his long, shaggy hair. On nice days, he often took their class to Castle Mountain for picnic lunches. There, under the flowering trees, he would tell his students thrilling tales about the mountains he'd climbed and the cities he'd visited. He would also describe his favorite books, like *The Diary of Anne Frank* and *The Broken Commandment,*

and Junko and the others would cry at the sad parts, even if they didn't totally understand them.

Mr. Watanabe was just about the smartest person she knew. If *he* believed she could hike to the top of a mountain, then she could hike to the top of a mountain. *Right?*

CHAPTER TWO

M r. Watanabe kept his promise. That summer, he took Junko and some of her classmates to the Nasu mountain range in Nikkō National Park.

They rode a train and a bus to get to their destination. Junko stared out the window at the blur of houses and farms they passed by. She had never traveled this far from home, so everything about the journey was exciting and new: the man selling *bento* box lunches at the train station, the leathery smell of the bus seats, the pretty countryside.

They finally reached the base of the mountain range. Junko couldn't believe how enormous

it was. It made Castle Mountain seem like an anthill! There were lots of other visitors there, too, carrying backpacks and walking sticks, just like they were.

After a quick snack of clementines, rice crackers, and barley tea, the group from Miharu headed for the mountainside inn where they would spend the night; the big hike to the top of Asahi Peak wasn't until tomorrow.

As they neared the inn, Hideo called out: "Hey, check it out. The ground is warm!"

Junko knelt down and touched the ground. It *was* warm, and not just from the sun. The others knelt and touched the ground, too, gasping in awe.

"This mountain range is volcanic," Mr. Watanabe explained. "There's hot water running beneath the surface."

"Did you say *volcanic*? Will it erupt?" Junko asked.

"No, it won't erupt. But it has created *onsen*,

or hot springs, all over this place. Tourists come from everywhere to bathe in them."

Mr. Watanabe was right. Junko had thought only cold water ran in rivers, but this part of Japan had hot-water rivers (and hot-water ponds, too). The area was full of them, and in fact, there were several onsen outside their inn. Grown-ups sat in them, sipping drinks out of wooden cups and looking relaxed and happy.

That night at their inn, Junko's group cooked their own dinner. They had packed miso bean paste, rice, curry mix, and vegetables in their backpacks along with their clothes.

Junko had never cooked at home. But she found that she *loved* cooking, especially with her classmates. They peeled potatoes and carrots to make into a curry to serve over rice. They sliced eggplants to fry. They diced tomatoes for a salad. Who knew that something so simple could be so much fun?

After dinner, they all went for a soak in one of the onsen. As the steam rose around them and the stars glittered like diamonds in the night sky, Junko thought that she'd never felt more peaceful. This trip wasn't just about climbing a mountain. It was about being with her friends and enjoying nature together.

~

"Come on, Jun-chan!"

"You've got this!"

Junko stopped in the middle of the steep, rocky trail, gasping for breath. She bent down and grabbed her knees, and her sun hat fell to the ground. From above, her classmates shouted encouragingly.

She wiped her brow with the back of her hand. She wasn't sure she could do this. Her lungs hurt, her legs ached, and she could feel painful blisters forming on her feet under her

thin socks and running shoes. She couldn't move another step.

Also, why had she worn a dress? Pants would have been much more practical. She, Junko Ishibashi, was obviously not cut out for this mountaineering business. Mountaineering was for people who had strength and stamina. People who weren't small and weak. People who knew what to wear for the occasion.

"Did I ever tell you about the first time I climbed a mountain?"

Junko glanced up. Mr. Watanabe was trotting down the trail toward her as the rest of the group disappeared around a bend.

Junko shook her head, still gasping for breath.

"It was awful. I promised myself I would never climb another mountain again," said Mr. Watanabe. "I guess I didn't keep that promise," he added with a grin.

Junko stood up a little straighter as she

considered this. Mr. Watanabe was always so full of energy and enthusiasm. She couldn't imagine him ever feeling like she did now. Like giving up. Like making a U-turn back to the inn. Like soaking her extremely sore muscles in an onsen as she sobbed in embarrassment.

She waited for Mr. Watanabe to give her sympathy. But he didn't. Instead, he handed her a metal thermos. "Keep drinking and stay hydrated. And *ganbatte*! The view at the top will be worth it." He turned and jogged back up the trail to join the others.

Junko stood frozen in her spot. She didn't know what to do next.

Drink. Stay hydrated.

She could do that much. She unscrewed the thermos lid and took a long, cool, delicious swig. She'd emptied her own thermos long ago and hadn't realized how thirsty she was. Her breathing slowly returned to normal.

Ganbatte. Do your best.

Junko tipped her head up to the blue sky. Treetops, feathery white clouds, soaring birds— and somewhere up there was her goal.

Break's over, she told herself. She picked up her sun hat, boosted her backpack onto her shoulders, and started walking again.

An hour later, she stood on the summit—the highest point of the mountain—with the rest of her group. Junko felt as though she were at the top of the world. She spun around on her toes, taking in the view of the surrounding mountains, endless forests, and tiny towns way below. The air was different up here, crisp and cold even though it was summer, and the ground beneath her feet bubbled with hot-springs water.

I did it! I climbed a mountain!

Something inside her had shifted. She, Junko Ishibashi, had become a mountaineer.

CHAPTER THREE

Over the following years, Junko really wanted to climb more mountains. But things didn't exactly work out that way.

"Did you finish your homework?" Junko's mother asked one night as they washed dishes together after dinner. She wore a white apron dress over her clothes, and her black hair was tied back in a bun. Now that Junko was in seventh grade, she had a huge amount of homework to do every day.

"Sure," Junko lied.

"What about your English test?"

"What about it?"

"It's tomorrow, isn't it? Did you study for it?"

"Yes," Junko lied again.

She never used to lie to her parents. She used to care about doing well in school. But that was all before her older sister Chikako had died from a disease called leukemia. After that, school didn't seem to matter. Neither did telling the truth or following the rules or anything else.

Kiyo sighed. She scrubbed at a stubborn pot and lectured Junko about the importance of studying. Junko pretended to listen, but instead she sang a song in her head—the one about the bossy mother crow who fussed over her little crows: "Crow, why do you cry so much?"—and concentrated on drying the soup bowls with a cloth. From the next room came the sounds of her father's crackly radio. Her brothers and sisters were scattered throughout the house, no doubt doing their homework like good, responsible children.

~

Later that week at school, Junko's English teacher handed back the tests.

"You can do better than this," he said. "I don't know what's happened to you. You used to be an outstanding student."

Whatever, Junko wanted to say. She disliked this teacher, who was mean and always gave her a hard time. She grabbed her test from him and stuffed it into her book bag without looking at it.

But as she closed her bag, she happened to see the grade scrawled at the top of the test.

It was low.

Really low.

She gulped. Maybe she was carrying this not-studying business a little too far?

For the next English test, Junko decided to prepare. If she got a high grade on it, then maybe the annoying teacher would stop nagging her and leave her alone.

Junko *did* get a high grade on the next test.

But instead of leaving her alone, the teacher called her to the front of the class.

"How did you go from such a low grade on the last test to such a high grade on this one? You obviously cheated," he accused her.

"I did *not* cheat!"

"I don't believe you."

Junko couldn't stand the idea that this teacher, or anyone else, didn't believe in her.

From then on, she went back to her old studying habits. She took careful notes in her classes, did her homework on time, and prepared diligently for her tests. Especially her English tests. She wanted to prove to her teacher that she could get good grades on her own.

School is sort of like mountain climbing, Junko thought. *I just need to put one foot in front of the other, keep going, and not give up.*

~

Junko's new determination carried her through to her last year of high school. By then, she had a plan: go to college and maybe become a teacher (not like the mean English teacher, but like Mr. Watanabe). She liked books, so she thought teaching would be a good profession for her.

There was only one problem with her plan. Girls weren't really encouraged to attend college; instead, they were expected to get married and start a family as soon as possible. In Japan, sometimes a girl's parents might find a husband for her through an "arranged marriage," which meant that two families agreed for their adult son and adult daughter to meet, date, and marry each other. (Junko's older sister Fuchi had met and married her husband this way.)

Junko wasn't ready for marriage, arranged or not. She wanted to learn things, experience the world, and enjoy her independence. She was meant to do something with her life—maybe teaching, maybe something else. College would give her the chance to figure out her future.

"You need to get married," her mother told her as her high school graduation neared. "Or you could get a job first. The Yamadas' daughter met her husband at the hospital where she worked as a receptionist. He's a doctor!"

"I don't want to get married right away. Or maybe ever. I want to have a career and make my own money," Junko replied.

Kiyo gasped. "What do you mean you don't want to get married right away or maybe ever? That's no kind of attitude for a—"

"Teaching is a perfectly acceptable profession for a woman," Junko's father interrupted. "More and more girls are going to college these days. Junko could apply to one of the nearby universities and—"

"I want to go to college in Tokyo," Junko cut in.

Morinobu stared at her. "You want to go to

college in Tokyo," he repeated.

"Absolutely not!" Kiyo exclaimed. "Tokyo is too far away. Besides, you're a country girl. You'd never survive in the city!"

"Fuchi lives there," Junko pointed out.

"Yes, with her *husband.*"

The argument went back and forth for weeks. In the end, Junko finally managed to convince her father to let her go to college in Tokyo, and once he was on her side, her mother agreed, too— although not for the right reasons.

"You'll find a nice husband in college," she told Junko. "The Sugimotos' daughter met her husband at the University of Tokyo, and he's a very successful lawyer now!"

"Uh-huh, okay, sure," Junko said to appease her.

Later, as Junko filled out her college applications, she thought about what her life would be like in Tokyo. She'd never been there, but Fuchi had told her many stories about the big, glamorous city. Junko looked forward to the hustle and bustle, the lively crowds. She looked forward to having coffee in fancy cafés and attending plays and concerts.

She also looked forward to maybe, just maybe, climbing a few mountains on the weekends once she had more freedom. Her dream of doing more mountaineering had faded since that first field trip with Mr. Watanabe, but it had never completely gone away.

Now, though, Junko's future seemed wide-open and full of possibilities. She was practically an adult. She was 100 percent (okay, maybe 99 percent) ready for college, for Tokyo...for all of it.

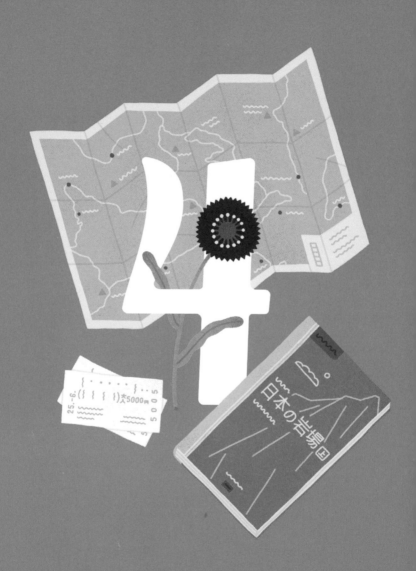

CHAPTER FOUR

On Junko's first day at Showa Women's University, she stood frowning at the campus map in a large courtyard. She couldn't figure out how to get to her next class.

"Excuse me," she said, trying to get the attention of the nearest person to ask for directions. Everyone seemed to be in a hurry.

A girl stopped. She wore a green silk dress that was belted at the waist and high-heeled black boots. She looked like a model from a fashion magazine.

Suddenly self-conscious, Junko touched the collar of her plain white cotton blouse. It was a hand-me-down from one of her sisters, and so was her old blue skirt with the holes in the pockets.

The girl's gaze traveled from Junko's hair (her mother had cut it with a pair of crafting scissors, so her bangs were a little crooked) to her leather shoes (they were also hand-me-downs and were badly scuffed) and back up again. She raised her perfectly groomed eyebrows.

"Yes?"

"Um…I'm new here," Junko stammered.

"Obviously. What's your accent? I mean, where are you from?"

Junko hadn't expected that question. Did her Japanese sound different from other people's Japanese? "I'm from Miharu."

"*Where?*"

"It's in the Tohoku region. In Fukushima Prefecture."

"Well, I've never heard of it."

Junko was so flustered that she forgot to ask for directions. The girl shrugged, then left to join two

other girls. They also looked like models.

I don't belong here, she thought miserably. *I should have stayed in the country, just like my mother said.*

Things didn't get any better after that first day. College seemed like a private club where everyone knew how to act except for her. The students were so stylish and sophisticated. And Junko's Japanese, with its rural accent, *did* sound different from other people's Japanese. Not to mention that she found her classes very difficult. The teachers were incredibly strict and serious. And college homework was much worse than middle and high school homework.

Plus, there was dormitory life.

"Junko, it's after ten pm. You know the rules. Lights out!" her dormitory mother scolded her. She made her rounds through the building every night to make sure all the students were in bed.

"But I'm not done with my homework for

tomorrow," Junko protested.

"You should have finished it during the day like everyone else. Lights out and into bed *now*. You're disturbing your dorm mates with your noise."

Noise? You mean the noise from me silently reading my history textbook? Junko wanted to say. *Or the noise from me silently solving math problems in my workbook?* But she knew better than to talk back; she'd get into even more trouble that way.

The other dormitory rules didn't make much sense, either.

"Junko, you know you're not allowed to leave the campus!"

"But I was only gone for fifteen minutes. I was hungry, and the cafeteria was closed, and—"

"How many times do I need to tell you? You're only allowed to leave the campus on Wednesdays, Saturdays, and Sundays."

Seriously?

Junko felt like a prisoner.

She was nervous and sad all the time because of the pressure and her loneliness. She couldn't sleep or eat, and she worried constantly about little things.

Concerned, her father came to Tokyo and brought her to a doctor. The doctor recommended that she take some time off from school. He told her that she had to rest and recharge and that she needed to take care of herself physically, mentally, and emotionally.

Junko listened to his advice and took a short leave of absence from Showa. She went to stay at an onsen resort and took long walks through the woods every day, which helped with her moods. She wrote in her diary, trying to sort through her jumbled feelings.

~

The break was exactly what Junko needed, and she returned to Showa to continue with her classes with a new perspective. She made some changes, like living in a rented room in a house instead of living in a dormitory. This gave her more freedom from strict curfews. She enjoyed music, so she started learning to play the koto, a harp-like Japanese instrument. She also tried harder to make friends and to have a life outside of school.

One day, some students invited her to go mountain climbing with them. The plan was to hike up Mount Mitake, near Tokyo. Of course, Junko agreed.

Hiking up Mount Mitake, Junko remembered how she'd felt hiking up Asahi Peak with Mr. Watanabe and her classmates. She remembered how hard it was on the way up, and how she'd almost quit and turned back around. She remembered the exhilaration and sense of achievement she had felt when she'd finally reached the summit.

On the way home, Junko went to a bookstore and bought a guidebook about the mountains in the area. She was excited to find that there were many high peaks near Tokyo. And she wanted to climb them all!

Using the guidebook, Junko began to organize weekend mountaineering trips for herself. Just planning these trips—choosing the mountains, buying train and bus tickets, looking over trail maps, packing her backpack—gave her a sense of joy and purpose. Her father sent her an allowance every month that helped to cover the costs. He believed that hiking was good for Junko, inside and out.

With these trips, Junko found a way back to herself. If she was feeling low, she could lift herself up by going to the mountains. She understood that each time she climbed, she would arrive at a wonderful place she had never been to before.

But her newfound happiness didn't last. One

day, she received a terrible—and unexpected—
telegram from her mother.

"Father passed away. Come home immediately."

~

"Your father would want you to finish college,"
Junko's mother told her after the funeral. She
wore her dark-colored mourning kimono, and her
hair seemed more silver than black.

Fresh tears spilled down Junko's cheeks. She'd
been crying so much that her eyeballs felt raw.
She guessed that her mother's eyes must feel raw,
too, even though Kiyo was doing her best to keep
her face calm and composed.

"College tuition is expensive," Junko said. "I
should come home and get a job and help pay the
bills, now that…now that…" Her voice caught in
her throat, and she began crying even harder.

"Your brothers and I will make sure our family
has enough money. We'll send you an allowance

every month, just as your father did."

"But I can't—"

"Yes, you can. No arguments. Now, go help your sisters make tea."

That night, Junko lay in her old, familiar bed, still dressed from the day, and stared up at the ceiling. The collar of her black dress felt too small, and her tights itched, but she barely noticed. She couldn't believe her father was gone. Who would encourage her to take care of herself…achieve her dreams…climb more mountains?

She planned to spend the rest of the week with her family and then take a train back to Tokyo to resume her classes. Thinking about Tokyo made her think even more about her father. He'd brought her to Tokyo for the very first time, at the beginning of her freshman year. On the journey, he'd told her about his own younger days. He'd ridden a motorcycle and played the violin. He'd loved adventure and trying new things.

Just like her.

Junko knew that she would carry her father's spirit with her for the rest of her life.

It's up to me now.

CHAPTER FIVE

"*Junko* is coming with us? Seriously? Are you sure she's ready?"

At the train station in Tokyo, a man named Yajima was complaining to his friend Yoko-o about her as though she were invisible. The two men were members of the Ryoho Climbing Club, a new mountaineering group that Junko had recently joined. Yoko-o was the leader of Ryoho. He was tall and had long, tousled hair that reminded Junko of her old teacher, Mr. Watanabe, except way younger. Yajima, also young, was short and stocky.

I'm standing right here, guys, Junko wanted to say. But she knew she should probably keep her mouth shut; she didn't want to make Yajima even *more* annoyed that a newcomer was climbing with them. A *female* newcomer.

"She'll be fine. I don't climb with anyone who's not ready. Grab your gear, both of you, or we're going to miss the 10:12 train," Yoko-o said impatiently.

Junko smiled sweetly at Yajima. He scowled at her but said nothing. *One point for female mountaineers!* she thought.

She didn't tell Yajima (or Yoko-o, either) that she'd been *this close* to not showing up. She'd agreed to perform at a koto recital earlier, and there was no way she could do both. But in the end, she'd thought, *Why not?* And so she'd performed at the recital, hastily changed from her fancy kimono into her climbing clothes, and made a mad dash for the train station.

Ryoho was the second mountaineering club Junko had belonged to since graduating from

Showa Women's University in 1962. During the day, she worked as an editor at the University of Tokyo. It wasn't her dream job, but it was nice to make money for herself. On the weekends, she tried to climb as often as possible with her fellow club members.

For years, Junko had heard that clubs were the best way to meet other mountaineers, learn new climbing skills, and save time and money on trips and equipment. But it hadn't been easy to find a club that would accept her. Most of them said "NO WOMEN ALLOWED" in their ads in big, bold letters.

The first club she'd joined *did* accept women, but they weren't happy about it. The male climbers gossiped behind the female climbers' backs, whispering things like, *So-and-so is only here to find a husband. So-and-so is always climbing with him, so they must be dating.* It was like fourth grade all over again.

Luckily for Junko, Yoko-o, who was the leader of Ryoho, was different from the guys at in her first club. He didn't seem to care that she was a woman; to him, she was just another mountaineer. Like her father (and Mr. Watanabe, too), Yoko-o seemed only to care that she was eager to learn and willing to train hard and not give up.

A few hours later, Junko, Yoko-o, and Yajima reached the base of Mount Tanigawa.

"You know Tanigawa is dangerous, right?" Yajima said casually to Junko as they left the train station and started toward the trailhead with their backpacks. "Hundreds of climbers have died here. One slip of the foot, or being at the wrong place at the wrong time during an avalanche, and…" He shrugged and made a grim face.

"Yajima…" Yoko-o warned.

"H-hundreds of people?" Junko repeated nervously. Okay, so maybe she *wasn't* ready for this.

"We'll be fine. Just remember your training.

Lean out. Don't climb with your arms. Avoid wet grass, which can be worse than a slippery rock face. Watch what I do, and listen to my instructions," Yoko-o said.

Junko nodded and took a deep, calming breath. She reminded herself of something that her father had taught her: *It's all right to be afraid. Fear is human. Just pay attention to what your fear is telling you and make smart decisions.*

These days, fear was a necessary part of mountaineering for Junko. Since her college graduation, she'd also graduated to a new kind of climbing. She no longer simply walked up trails, flat or steep; she'd added rock climbing to her skill set.

Rock climbing is the sport of climbing up, down, or across rocks, with the goal being to reach the top (and return to the bottom) without falling. It involves breaking your climb up into a series of steps—for example, placing two anchors (one way above, one way below) on the ledges of a steep, sometimes vertical rock face; tying a long rope between them; and using that rope to climb securely. These steps have to be repeated as you and the rest of your team go up or down.

As a climber, you have to trust the people you are climbing with to decide on a route, to change that route along the way if you run into problems, to rope or not to rope, and make the dozens of other decisions—big and small—that have to be made during a climb.

I would trust Yoko-o with my life, Junko thought as they started up Mount Tanigawa. *And, to be honest, I trust Yajima, too. He may be kind of a jerk, but he's a good climber.*

~

The climb up Mount Tanigawa that day was successful. Junko continued climbing with the Ryoho club and learning from Yoko-o.

At a club meeting one evening, he pulled her aside.

"You're ready to go to eight thousand meters now," he told her quietly. Eight-thousand-meter mountains were some of the highest mountains in the world.

"I don't think so…"

"Of course you are. You're also ready to climb alone with a female partner."

Alone with a female partner?

Female climbers were still rare compared to male climbers. Because of that, the best, most experienced climbers tended to be men. And when you were still learning, it was important to climb with someone better and more experienced than yourself for safety reasons. If women were new to climbing, it followed that a woman shouldn't climb alone with another woman…right?

"You're ready, Junko. Okay, let's get back to club business."

Yoko-o was a person of few words, and he never gave compliments.

But he was giving her a compliment now.

Eight thousand meters. Female partner.

She was ready!

CHAPTER SIX

One day, Junko got an unexpected call at work.

"Hi! My name is Rumie," said a woman's voice. "I'd love to climb with you sometime. Do you want to meet up and plan a trip?"

Junko was intrigued by this woman's invitation, especially after Yoko-o's encouraging words. The two women agreed to meet at the train station in Tokyo the following week.

Junko got there first and waited in the lobby area. She stood off to the side to avoid the mad rush of commuters who all looked alike in their black and gray suits, hats, and briefcases. The delicious smells of freshly baked *pan*—sweet, custard-filled buns—wafted from a nearby snack stand, but she wasn't hungry. In fact, her stomach kind of hurt, and her palms were sweaty. She wasn't used to strangers inviting her to climb with them. What if she didn't like this woman? What if the woman didn't like Junko? What if Yoko-o was wrong, and Junko wasn't ready to climb without an experienced male climber along?

"Jun-chan!"

Only her family, a few of her friends, and other climbers in her club used this nickname for her. Junko looked around to see who had called out, but she didn't see anyone she knew.

Then a young woman came running up to her, waving like mad. She stopped in front of Junko, a wide smile on her round face. She was almost the same height as Junko, and her hair was shaggy. Both young women were small but strong.

"Sorry for surprising you! I'm Rumie!" the woman began breathlessly. "I've seen you on some

of the weekend trains to the mountains, and I
overheard other people calling you Jun-chan,
so I said it without thinking. But I will call you
'Junko-san' from now on, like a person with
manners. I promise! I'm so, so happy to meet you!"

Why had Junko been so nervous? Rumie was
friendly and warm.

"I'm happy to meet you, too! And it's okay—
please call me Jun-chan."

Rumie smiled even wider. "Jun-chan, then."

At a nearby café, they talked about mountains
over cups of coffee and plates of *pan*.

"How often do you climb? Like every
weekend?" Junko asked Rumie.

"More! Every weekend, and during the
week, too," Rumie replied. "I take a train to the
mountains as soon as my workday is over. Then I
climb up, camp out, climb back down, and take a
train to Tokyo the next morning so I won't be late
for my job."

"Are you *serious*?"

Rumie grinned from ear to ear. "I guess I'm a little obsessed with climbing."

"A *little*?"

The two women cracked up.

"I'm jealous you can do that, though," Junko admitted. "So have you ever climbed with a female partner?"

"Nope. You'd be my first. What about you?"

"You'd be my first, too. Yoko-o-san said he thought I was ready to climb with a female partner."

"*The* Yoko-o-san? He's a megalegend. Did you know he had a terrible climbing accident when he was a teenager?"

"What?"

"He and another climber. At Tsuitate Slab. Yoko-o-san was in the hospital for a long time."

"Oh my gosh!"

Junko thought about Yoko-o. Knowing he hadn't given up on mountaineering after experiencing such a tragedy and being hurt himself made her admire him even more.

"He's one of my heroes," Rumie said, nodding slowly. "But you know what? So are you. Everyone says you're an awesome climber. You're a woman, and you're small, but you don't let that stop you."

"You're a woman, and you're small, too," Junko pointed out.

Rumie laughed. "True. Okay, so we're *both* heroes. Now, what are you doing on Saturday? Whatever it is, clear your calendar, because I have *the* best climbing route planned on Mount Tanigawa…"

~

"Why can't you come home this weekend? Everyone will be here to celebrate your aunt's birthday except for you," Kiyo chided Junko over the phone some time later.

"I promised my friend Rumie I'd go climbing with her. We already bought our train tickets," Junko replied. Even though she hated disappointing her family, she wasn't about to give up a climbing trip to Mount Tanigawa. Sure, she and Rumie had made that trip almost every weekend since they'd met—but that didn't count, since each trip involved a different part of the mountain and a different route.

"You're not doing anything risky, are you? You girls are just going on a nice, gentle hike up one of those easy trails with the pretty views?" Kiyo asked worriedly.

"Of course!" Junko lied. Kiyo would be upset if she knew the kinds of mountains she and Rumie climbed or realized they no longer went on nice, gentle hikes but up steep rock faces. Climbers could die, especially on a difficult, dangerous mountain like Mount Tanigawa.

"*Well*...all right. But I would like to see you soon. I was thinking of taking the train to Tokyo next weekend to visit you."

Next weekend. Junko and Rumie already had another climbing adventure planned. But her mother might not be so understanding about *two* mountaineering trips in a row. Junko's family had no idea that almost all her free time was taken up by climbing these days. She didn't want to change her plans.

"Oh, wow, sorry! I'm, um...There's an important conference at the university, and they need me to work. Maybe next month?"

"*Another* conference? You're working much too hard. How will you ever find a husband when you're working all the time?" Kiyo still hadn't given up on the idea of a husband for Junko, preferably an arranged-marriage husband. "And speaking of husbands...Mrs. Morimoto and I were talking the other day. Her son Hiroshi is your age, and he's an accountant. *And* he's single! We thought the two of you might like each other!"

"Oops, there's someone at the door. I have to go!" Junko fibbed.

"Jun-chan!"

"I'll call you again soon, bye! I love you!"

Junko hung up, suddenly feeling guilty and anxious. She didn't like deceiving her mother. And Kiyo wasn't wrong to worry about the risks of climbing.

But along with the guilt and anxiety, Junko felt a sense of exhilaration. She thought about her trip to Mount Tanigawa this coming weekend with Rumie. Mountaineering was her passion, and she wasn't about to stop because of her mother's (or anyone else's) old-fashioned attitudes about what women should or shouldn't do.

She thought about Mr. Watanabe's words to her during that long-ago field trip.

Ganbatte. Do your best.

I'm going to continue doing my best, mountain after mountain, she promised him silently.

7

"See him?" Rumie said to Junko in a low voice.

Junko glanced at the handsome young guy walking down the train platform. Black bangs peeked out from under a red cap. He wore blue hiking pants, red boots, and a bright-blue jacket. A big brown backpack was slung across his back.

"That's Masanobu Tabei," Rumie continued. "He's like a celebrity in the climbing world. The train conductors always save seats for him and his friends way in the front."

"Because...?"

"Because then, when the train arrives at the

mountain, they can get off first and beat everyone else to the trailhead."

"Wow," Junko said, impressed. It was a general rule in mountaineering that at the start of any chosen route, one climbing party went up at time, while others waited to go up a little later to avoid overcrowding. Being the first party meant that you had a quiet, unspoiled climb all to yourselves, at least until others caught up with you.

"What club does he belong to?" she asked Rumie.

"The Honda Climbing Club."

"Have you ever met him?"

"What? No! I'd be too nervous to talk to him!"

"Really?"

Junko couldn't imagine Rumie being nervous about talking to anyone; she was always so bubbly and outgoing.

Their train finally reached Mount Tanigawa. For that day's climb, Junko and Rumie had chosen a route they'd never taken before: the South Ridge of the Ichinokura-sawa area. By coincidence, it turned out that Masanobu and his friends had chosen that one, too.

Of course, Masanobu's party had a major head start over Junko and Rumie, thanks to the train conductor. As the two women climbed a particularly difficult rock face, Junko focused on the tasks at hand: place the anchor, tie the rope, repeat. She never took safety for granted. She knew that one little slip could mean the difference between life and death.

Still, once in a while, she caught sight of Masanobu up above, and she paused to watch him climb. She noticed that he ascended steep rock faces at the same steady pace that he walked on flat trails. He seemed so confident, so sure of himself. *I'll climb like that, too, someday*, Junko thought.

Hours into their climb, Junko spotted Masanobu taking a break in a snowy clearing. Even after years of mountaineering, she was still always amazed by the sight of snow in May. Masanobu sat alone on a big boulder, busy with a task. Was he tying a rope? Examining an anchor?

No, she realized as she got closer. He was making dessert out of canned sweet adzuki beans and fresh snow. Junko almost laughed in surprise.

Masanobu glanced up at the exact same moment. *Oh, great, he caught me staring at him*, Junko thought, her cheeks flushing with embarrassment.

He waved to Junko. "Hello! Would you like some?"

The famous Masanobu Tabei was inviting her to have a snack with him.

What should I do?

Rumie had been crouched down on the ground, tying and retying her hiking boots. Now, as she stood up, her gaze bounced between Junko and Masanobu.

She grinned and elbowed Junko. "I'll just

be over there, putting on more sunscreen," she whispered, nodding to a boulder on the other side of the clearing. "Go talk to him!"

"You already put on sunscreen. You have to come with me!" Junko whispered back.

"I think he wants to talk to you alone. 'Kay, bye!"

"*Rumie!*"

Junko wasn't used to spending time with men she didn't know. But she couldn't be rude, could she? *Courage,* she told herself. *If I can climb Mount Tanigawa, I can have a five-minute conversation with a cute guy.*

She took a deep breath and walked over to Masanobu. He was even more handsome up close. She sat down and nervously twisted her gloved hands in her lap.

"We've never met. I'm Masanobu Tabei," he said.

"Hi! I'm Junko Ishibashi."

"I was watching you earlier. You're a very skilled climber."

That was *huge* praise, coming from him. He didn't even add *for a woman*, which was doubly huge. "Thank you! I've heard you're a rock star in the climbing world," she said.

"I'm not a rock star—I just enjoy rocks."

Junko laughed. The legendary Masanobu Tabei was funny *and* modest.

He handed her a tin cup full of snow and adzuki beans. "Here you go. It's sort of an instant snow cone. As you can see, I'm an excellent cook!" he joked.

"You're not a typical Japanese man, then."

"No, I'm not. Actually, I like cooking. For real. I make killer *gyoza*, and my miso soup isn't bad, either."

"I could go for some dumplings and miso soup right now. It's freezing up here!"

"This snow cone is probably not the right thing to serve you, then. Sorry."

Junko held the tin cup carefully and brought it

up to her lips. It was difficult to hold it with her padded cold-weather hiking gloves, but she didn't want to remove them, either.

She took a bite. "It's really yummy. Thank you for sharing it with me!"

"Sure, any time."

Junko smiled as she continued eating the snow cone. She'd made a new friend. With a guy. With a *famous* guy, at least in the climbing world, which was the only world that really mattered to her.

That wasn't so hard, she thought.

From across the clearing, she saw Rumie giving her a double thumbs-up through her thick hiking gloves.

~

After that day, Junko and Masanobu ran into each other more and more—on mountains, on trains, on buses, even on the busy streets of Tokyo. It was as though the universe was trying to bring them together.

Since they belonged to different clubs, they never climbed together. Another general rule in mountaineering was that you should only climb with members of your own club; in fact, Rumie had quit her club and joined the Ryoho Climbing Club so that she and Junko could climb as a pair without getting into trouble.

Still, one day, Masanobu said to Junko: "The south face of Tanigawa is really nice in the fall. Lots of colorful leaves…We should climb it together to see."

Junko couldn't say yes fast enough. She really liked Masanobu!

~

Two years later, on the day of their wedding, Junko Ishibashi became Junko Tabei. It was Japanese law for a woman to take her husband's name.

"You may be Junko Tabei now, but I don't

want you to be some sort of traditional Japanese housewife," Masanobu told her on their honeymoon. "I want you to keep climbing higher and higher mountains, and I want to help you do that."

Junko knew she had found the perfect partner for her.

CHAPTER EIGHT

I n September of 1967, Junko and Masanobu were in Miharu to honor the seventh anniversary of her father's passing. She'd skipped a weekend climbing trip with Rumie to be with her family.

"I'll go with Yamazaki and Yoshimura, then. They said they're free," Rumie had told her.

"But you hardly know them, and that's a dangerous ascent," Junko had pointed out. "Why don't you wait till I get back, and we can go next weekend instead?"

"Seriously, I'll be fine!"

A few days later, Junko received a telegram from Rumie's mother that said, "Rumie is missing on Mount Tanigawa. Come as soon as possible."

Dread spread through Junko's body.

No, no, no. Please let my best friend be safe! she prayed.

She and Masanobu wasted no time. They changed into their climbing clothes, packed their ropes and anchors and other gear, and caught the first train to Mount Tanigawa. They also contacted as many climbing friends as possible to help find Rumie.

By the time Junko and Masanobu reached Mount Tanigawa, the search and rescue effort was already underway, led by Yoko-o and the rest of the Ryoho Climbing Club. Rumie's mother was inside a building at the base, waiting for news.

"You go join the others. I'll stay here with her mom," Junko told Masanobu.

He nodded wordlessly and rushed off with his backpack. Junko put her arm around Rumie's mother, who was pale and shaking.

"What if they don't find her? Or what if they find her and she's already dead?"

"Rumie's a great climber. She's probably just camping somewhere," Junko reassured her friend's mother.

"I hope you're right!"

But six hours later, the news came back that Yoko-o had found Rumie. She hadn't survived.

Masanobu explained what happened. "Rumie, Yamazaki, and Yoshimura were descending from the summit when Yamazaki lost her footing on a slippery rock face and started to fall," he said, his voice heavy. "Rumie reached over to try to catch her, but in the process, she lost her footing and started to fall, too. By some miracle, Yamazaki's backpack strap caught on a tree branch and broke her fall. But our poor Rumie wasn't so lucky."

Junko couldn't believe it. Her best friend—her sweet, bubbly, unstoppable best friend—was gone.

~

Rumie's death left a hole in Junko's life. For a long time, she couldn't bring herself to climb a mountain, any mountain. But she eventually started climbing again, in honor of her best friend's memory. She joined up with a group of female climbers and formed an all-women's club, the Ladies Climbing Club. With them, Junko climbed her first overseas mountain, Annapurna III, which is in the Himalayas in Asia.

Then, in 1970, they came up with a spectacular new plan. Junko told Masanobu about it over dinner in their one-room apartment, which was furnished with a few futons, an old desk, and some other pieces of beat-up furniture. It was not a palace, but it was home, and the two of them were happy there.

"The Ladies Climbing Club is planning to climb Mount Everest," Junko announced.

Masanobu gasped, almost spitting out his ramen noodles. "That's incredible! Wow, congratulations! You'll be the first women ever to ascend the highest mountain in the world!"

"That is, *if* we succeed, of course. But we need to talk about it first, Masanobu, because we'll have to give up a lot. I'll be training and preparing for at least a year. It's going to cost a fortune, too, so each club member has to raise money *plus* contribute their own, and you and I aren't exactly rich. There's tons of paperwork to fill out to get permission from the government of Nepal. And if our application is approved, I'll be gone for at least six months…or forever, if something happens…"

Junko's words trailed off as she thought about Rumie.

Masanobu held Junko's hands in his own. "Nothing's going to happen. You're the best climber I know."

"Stop," Junko said, blushing.

"Seriously. You're ready for this. It's what you were meant to do."

"Do you think so?"

"I do. I have only one request."

"What's that?"

"Could we have a baby first, before you leave, so I'll have someone to keep me company?"

A baby. Junko loved the idea of starting a family. Still, how would she be able to take care of a child—or children—and continue climbing mountains? It wasn't just weekend train rides to Mount Tanigawa anymore. Her excursions with the Ladies Climbing Club took up weeks, sometimes months. And Mount Everest would be the most time-consuming, demanding, and

dangerous trip of her life.

As though reading her mind, Masanobu said: "It's okay. Remember, I'm not a typical Japanese man. I'd be happy to stay home and take care of our little family while you go off on your adventures."

"Really?"

"Really."

In 1969, Masanobu had lost several toes to frostbite while climbing in the Italian and Swiss Alps with friends. Junko knew this had slowed him down a bit, but not entirely. She understood that his offer to let her go to Mount Everest came from his love for her and from his generous spirit.

Junko hugged him. "Okay. A baby, then Everest. No big deal, right?"

"It will be a piece of cake," Masanobu said with a wink.

They both laughed.

CHAPTER NINE

"Did you pack your ropes?" Masanobu asked Junko. It was almost time to leave for the airport.

"Yes."

"Dehydrated miso and soy sauce?"

"Got it."

"Toilet paper?"

"Affirmative."

"What about extra gloves? You know you'll need a lot of extra gloves, don't you?"

"Did I tell you that the women and I made gloves out of car covers? Do we know how to save money, or what?"

Masanobu smiled, but he looked tired. In the past few months, he'd spent many late nights taking care of their daughter, Noriko, who was almost three, while working at his day job at the Honda Motor Company. They lived in a house now, in the countryside just outside of Tokyo.

Noriko was taking a nap in the next room. Junko's heart felt heavy at the thought of having to leave her.

"I'm going to miss her birthday. I'm an awful mother!"

"You're a wonderful mother. Plus, we had an early birthday party for her, remember?"

Masanobu wrapped his arms around her. "Don't worry about us. We'll be fine," he said. "Focus on yourself and your team. Complete your mission with all your heart."

"Thank you," Junko whispered back. She'd been trying not to cry, but now tears spilled down her face.

"Why are you crying?"

"I'm happy, but I'm also sad. I don't want to leave you two—and you're the most wonderful husband in the world."

Masanobu held her tighter.

Junko finally forced herself to say goodbye and left for the airport. *One foot in front of the other,* she thought.

On the plane, Junko felt emotionally exhausted. She thought about the epic journey ahead—Calcutta, then Kathmandu, then the base of Everest, then Everest itself, which would involve many complicated maneuvers in brutally cold weather with no guarantee of safety or success. She also thought about Noriko and Masanobu. Would they be okay without her? Would she be okay without them?

She gazed out at the clouds outside the tiny, round airplane window.

Complete your mission with all your heart.

She repeated Masanobu's words to herself over and over.

~

By May 4, 1975, Junko and her group had been on Mount Everest for a month and a half. The fourteen members of the Ladies Climbing Club hadn't undertaken the journey alone. At various points on their travels to—and up—Mount Everest, they'd been accompanied by porters, support climbers, and a television crew of four reporters and three cameramen. The first all-female expedition on Mount Everest was big news. And it would be even bigger news if they succeeded.

Many of the porters and support climbers were Sherpa people. The Sherpas were members of an ethnic tribe that lived in the region, and they were known for their mountaineering skills.

Junko thought about Masanobu and Noriko every hour of every day, *especially* when she

was struggling to climb a particularly icy cliff or staring down into an endless empty space between two massive rock walls.

Complete your mission with all your heart.

At this point, she just wanted to complete her mission alive and go home to her family. She'd already missed Noriko's third birthday, although she had managed to draw a picture of a birthday cake on the back of a blank postcard and mail it from the Himalayas.

Junko was almost there. On May 4, the group was a week away from the summit. *Just seven more days, and we'll achieve our goal*, Junko thought as they pitched their tents for the night. There had been a mix-up, and her tent was missing a sleeping bag. So she and another woman were forced to share one. Only their legs fit inside, so they wrapped their down coats around the top halves of their bodies for warmth.

Cramped and cold, but tired from the day's

climb, Junko surrendered to the icy silence of the night and fell asleep instantly.

~

Junko awoke to a strange vibration. Was the ground beneath them trembling? Before she knew what was happening, there was a very loud noise—*WHAM!*—as several tons of snow and ice hit their camp. It was an avalanche.

Pressure fell against Junko's body. The tent began rolling helplessly with her and her tent mate still inside. Junko was tossed upside down, then right side up, then upside down again. Her brain was spinning, and she could hardly breathe. Was she about to die? Or was she already dead?

Then…*silence.* And stillness.

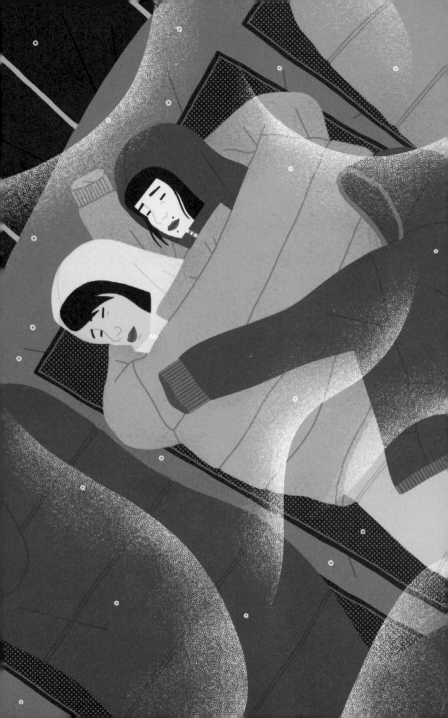

CHAPTER TEN

The avalanche stopped as abruptly as it had begun.

"Is everyone okay?" Junko cried out. There was no answer. She wondered in horror if she was the only one still alive.

Then she realized that there was a person on top of her. Her tent mate, Yuriko.

"Are you all right?" Junko demanded.

"Everything hurts," Yuriko replied in a ragged voice.

"We have to get out of here."

"How? We're trapped."

Yuriko was right. Their tent had been buried under big blocks of snow and ice. Junko tried to move, but it was impossible. There was no space between them and the tent walls.

Junko realized that they needed to cut their way out of the tent. She reached for the camping tool that she wore on a cord around her neck.

The tool contained a knife. She used her teeth to open the blade, but she couldn't move her arms enough to use it on the tent walls.

"Yuriko, take this knife!"

Yuriko's eyelids were fluttering. She was obviously about to black out. They were quickly running out of air.

"Yuriko!" Junko said, but her voice sounded far away.

Terrified, she tried to take a breath, but got nothing, just a dry wheezing in her throat.

Bright lights began to flash in front of her eyes.

No, no, no!

The last thought Junko had before she passed out was that she had to stay alive.

~

Junko woke to the sound of scared voices and the sensation of strong arms pulling on her.

"Where's the first aid kit?"

"We need to radio for help!"

"What if there's another avalanche?"

Slowly, Junko became aware of her surroundings. She was lying in a tent—an upright, intact tent—next to several of her teammates. The Sherpa support climbers were rushing around tending to injuries.

"Is everyone alive?" Junko managed to choke out.

"No one died," someone answered.

That was a miracle. The campsite had been buried by a huge wave of snow and ice.

Junko and the others spent several days recovering. They all wanted to continue up to the summit.

The team doctor tried to talk Junko into

quitting. "You're not in any shape to climb. You need to rest."

"I'll be good to go in two days. I'm not quitting."

Junko *didn't* quit. Over the following week, more team members gave up because of their injuries, sickness, or fatigue, and finally only she and one of the Sherpa support climbers, Ang Tsering, remained.

On May 16, 1975, twelve days after the avalanche, Junko reached the summit. She was surprised to find that it wasn't very big—just the size of one of the tatami mats she slept on at home.

"I made it!" she announced to the rest of the team on her walkie-talkie. She heard cheers and clapping and everyone shouting, *"Congratulations!"*

She had done it!

To commemorate her victory, Junko planted a Japanese flag and a Nepalese flag in the snow.

Many years after the Mount Everest expedition, Junko gave Mr. Watanabe, her fourth-grade teacher, a very special present for his seventieth birthday. She invited him to Nepal, where she chartered a private helicopter to fly

them to the Himalayas.

After thirty minutes in the air, Mount Everest came into view. Mr. Watanabe gasped in wonder.

"Thank you," he said quietly.

The moment was just as sweet as when she'd reached the summit in 1975.

AFTERWORD

After climbing Mount Everest, Junko Tabei became famous. She never felt like a celebrity, though. She thought of herself as a regular person who enjoyed climbing and who wanted to spread the word that everyone should try it for themselves—not to achieve fame and fortune, but to have a good time.

When their daughter, Noriko, was six years old, Junko and Masanobu welcomed a son, Shinya. Junko loved being a mother as much as she loved being a mountaineer.

Junko climbed mountains for the rest of her life. She climbed the highest peak in over seventy countries, and was the first woman to climb the Seven Summits (the seven highest peaks in the world).

Junko was also an activist. She knew about the negative impacts too much climbing had on

Mount Everest, like littering, water pollution, and the loss of trees. In 1990, she established the Himalayan Adventure Trust of Japan to help protect the mountain range.

In 2011, disaster struck in the Tohoku region, where Junko's hometown was located: an earthquake and a tsunami, followed by a terrible accident at a nuclear power plant. In response, Junko created Project Cheer Up Tohoku to help the area and its people. One of the projects was an annual trip for local high school students to climb Mount Fuji. This trip continues today. Junko's son, Shinya, who is also an avid mountaineer, has taken on his mother's role with the project and leads students to the top of Mount Fuji every summer.

In 2012, Junko was diagnosed with cancer. She lived for another four years and climbed mountains until her final days. She died on October 20, 2016, at the age of seventy-seven, with her family by her side.

Before she passed away, she asked her son to do three things for her:

1. Let everyone know about the wonders of nature.

2. Continue the Mount Fuji program for high school students.

3. Protect and take care of Masanobu and Noriko.

"Anyone can take up mountaineering," she told him. "I started out as a little girl with no athletic talent. I just wanted to challenge myself and have fun. And I did!"

ACTIVITIES

TYING KNOTS

You already know one knot — the kind you use to tie your shoes! But there are nearly 4,000 other unique knots with different purposes.

For instance, Junko and her fellow climbers used several different knots to keep them safe as they climbed high mountains. Tying a knot can come in handy in many situations. Grab an old shoelace, a piece of rope, or a string and practice tying the knots described below.

Climbers use a **Girth Hitch** knot to tie themselves to a fixed point, like a tree. It's used for rescues since it's quick and easy to tie. Here are the steps:

1. Place a rope loop behind the object you're attaching it to.

2. Pull the remaining loop away from object to tighten.

3. Wrap the open end over the object and feed it through the loop underneath.

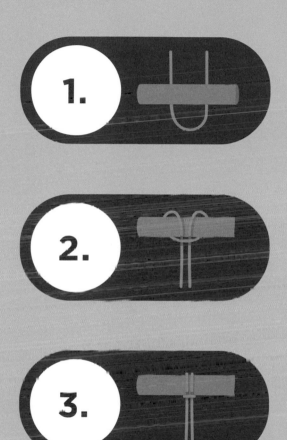

The **Figure Eight Follow Through** knot is one of the strongest knots and helps climbers connect securely to a wall. Here are the steps:

1. Make a figure "eight" with your rope.

2. Wrap the free end of the figure "eight" around the item you're tying yourself to.

3. Take the free end and follow the "eight" around a second time.

4. Then pull the end tight.

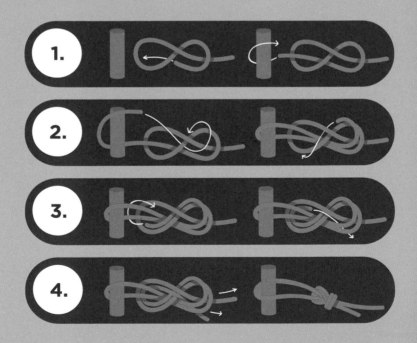

The **Double Overhand Stopper** knot is used at the end of a rope for extra security. This knot will make sure that a climber's rope never slips unexpectedly. Here are the steps:

1. Make a loop and feed one end into the loop.

2. Take the end and pass it through the loop one more time.

3. Pull the ends to tighten.

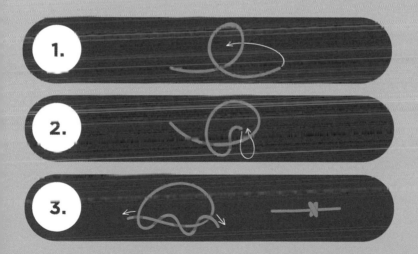

FINDING BALANCE

As a climber, it's important to strengthen your balancing skills, so that you feel confident climbing on less stable surfaces. Climbers have to switch out their hands and feet when reaching for their next hold, so they don't slip and fall. It is also important for them to shift their weight by leaning away or toward individual holds/footholds on the wall. Work on your balancing skills by trying the activity below!

1. Stick a long piece of masking tape on your floor in a straight line. Hold two tennis balls or similar-sized objects in each hand and walk along the tape, following the line. Holding the tennis balls will strengthen your grip while also helping you to improve your balance when you can't use your hands to steady yourself.

2. Put the tennis balls away and look for a softcover book. Now try walking along the tape while balancing the book on your head. It may help to have your arms spread out like an airplane!

CONQUERING FEARS

Climbing can be scary, which is how Junko felt the first time she tried it. However, she learned that trying new things can make you stronger. When you really focus on the task in front of you, something that used to be frightening won't seem very scary anymore.

Talk about a time you were scared to try something new but decided to try it anyway. What did you learn? What did you like or not like about that experience?

Is there something you've been too scared to try so far but would like to try someday?

Cotopaxi creates outdoor products that help alleviate poverty, move people to do good, and inspire adventure.

1% of Cotopaxi's revenue goes towards grants focused on providing basic needs to communities in the Americas.

Visit them at www.cotopaxi.com
or @cotopaxi

ACKNOWLEDGMENTS

While Junko Tabei may not have set out to be known as the first woman to climb Everest, there's no better example. Tabei's personal sacrifices and conservation efforts remind us that we are never too small to put one foot in front of the other and reach our highest potential.

Nancy Ohlin, you've really astounded us. We thank you. Montse Galbany, your passion for the mountains glimmers in every painstaking detail. Tabei comes alive at every page turn, and that is in no doubt thanks to your gorgeous illustrations. Thank you, too, to Martha Cipolla and Marisa Finkelstein for your thoughtful reads. Cotopaxi has been a generous partner

And finally, Rebel Girls would like to thank our readers. Your continued interest drives the mission further than we'd ever dreamed. Remember, what some see as weakness can actually be strength. Junko Tabei was always underestimated—and there's no greater advantage than being overlooked. Prove to the world and yourself that you are worthy.

ABOUT REBEL GIRLS

Rebel Girls is an award-winning cultural media engine founded in 2012, spanning over seventy countries. Through a combination of thought-provoking stories, creative expression, and business innovation, Rebel Girls is on a mission to balance power and create a more inclusive world. Rebel Girls is home to a diverse and passionate group of rebels who work in Los Angeles, New York, Atlanta, Merida (Mexico), London, and Milan.

Find Rebel Girls online (rebelgirls.co), on Facebook (Facebook.com/rebelgirls), Instagram (@rebelgirls), and Twitter (@rebelgirlsbook).